I0731143

The
Nanny
Diaries

#1

ISBN: 9781952422102
First Printing, 2020

DarlingCoxx@gmail.com
Instagram: @DarlingCoxx
OnlyFans: @DarlingCoxx

Chapter One

Dear Diary,

Tonight was a cluster fuck of epic proportions. I have a very stressful job interview tomorrow. My parents insist that I shouldn't work while going to college. They say my studies need to be my primary focus. Bless them. I know they mean well, but we're not exactly rich either. I would like to have my own spending money, and it would be nice to pay some of my tuition expenses outright. Already, the student loans from just my first semester will have me in hock until retirement.

As I was saying, this job

interview is at the infamous Wyndham estate. Everyone within a hundred miles of here knows the name Wyndham. He has his hands in everything, and is worth more than I can count. He needs a nanny. My pre-interview to screen me over the phone laid out some of the basics. It was full time pay with part time work. Since the children were in school during the day, it'd leave me free to attend class and do my own homework.

What I don't understand and forgot to ask was just who would I be caring for exactly? As far as I was aware, Mr. Wyndham's children were grown. His wife did pass away not long ago. He probably married some barely legal supermodel and got her knocked up as most fiftyish men of wealth are known to do.

This job would be a blessing for me all the way around. It scheduled nicely with college which would make my parents happy. The pay was unbelievable. Plus, one of the perks was I would get to live in the guest house! My boyfriend Jake and I hardly ever get any real privacy. That alone would be worth it to me to take this job.

My parents were supposed to go out to dinner tonight which meant Jake and I would have the house to ourselves for a couple hours to destroy each other's bodies. I needed the release now more than ever. A good fuck session would release my stress and anxiety over this interview leaving me relaxed and calm for tomorrow.

Except my mom twisted her ankle as they were leaving the house. She slipped on a step walking down off the porch. Dad's eyesight leaves him not fit to drive at night, so I was the one who drove them to the emergency room. It didn't take long there which was a surprise, but they obviously stayed home afterward instead of going out like they had planned.

I couldn't even run out to hook up with Jake on a dark country road in the back of his car. I had to stay home and act as mom's nurse maid. I love her to death. Don't get me wrong. It's just that she was coming between me and sex.

Mom didn't go to bed until late, and Jake was already asleep. He has an early class three days a week including tomorrow. That meant if there was any hope of relieving my tension, it was in my hands. Literally.

Luckily, I already had my outfit picked out. I did that as soon as the agency called me about the position since I'd have to wear something classy and professional. I didn't even own anything that would suffice. I had to borrow an outfit from a friend. That was one less thing to worry about right now at least.

It was long past the time I had hoped to be in bed when I finally made my way up to my room. I went into the bathroom and turned on the shower. My parents' room is right next to mine, so it's the only way I feel secure that they can't hear the hum of my toys through the wall.

Stripping completely, I sat on the edge of the toilet for a minute playing with my pussy just to get everything warmed up. The steam from the shower helped set the mood as well. Once I was ready, I straddled the edge of the tub.

My preferred playmate was affectionately called Baby Blue. He was small, but big enough to do the trick. I never wanted to use anything too large that might stretch me out. Jake is rather partial to my tight pussy. I suctioned the dildo down to the edge of the tub then climbed on board. The cold of the silicone was a stark contrast to the heat of the shower running inches from me. It sent shivers throughout my body.

Then I picked up my favorite stim. It was small and white, but it packed a punch. I kept it hidden under my bed where it was always on the charger to make sure it was ready whenever I had an urge. And let's face it, that's pretty often considering the lack of opportunity for me and Jake to get together.

This little guy didn't have a name. I could never think of anything worthy enough for it. I turned it on the highest setting and just held it directly on my clit. I began grinding against Baby Blue while keeping the stim held firm. That is all it takes. About sixty seconds of it, and I'm already climaxing.

To be truthful, I don't even need the dildo. The stim alone brings me to orgasm, and I please myself that way often. But it's like eating Chinese food. You can get full, but you're hungry again soon because there's no substance to rice. That's how I feel about using stims. It does the trick, but it won't be long until I'm craving cock. I have to something in my pussy to be fully satisfied.

Most of the time, I do this quick. Just something to stave off the desires until I can be with Jake again. Not tonight. This time I rode Baby Blue until I feared I might break him in two. I welcomed release after release until I didn't have the energy to hold myself up on the edge of the tub anymore.

I stood up and began to clean everything up including myself. My legs shook and felt weak. I chuckled quietly marveling at how easily I can bring myself to the point of exhaustion when it took Jake months to figure out just what to do to please me completely.

It's not his fault. He was my first. I had never even touched myself before him. Jake bought me my first toy. Actually, he's bought me all of them. How was I supposed to teach him what I like when I didn't know myself?

In my room, I put Baby Blue away and was about to put the stim back on the charger when I changed my mind. Instead I took it to bed with me just in case I had trouble sleeping. I know I won't. That quick romp in the bathroom still has me drained.

Chapter Two

Dear Diary,

My interview was today for the nanny position at the Wyndham estate. It seems like an easy job, and I'm not really sure why a nanny is needed at all. Mr. Wyndham's wife died last month, and he's hiring a nanny to look after his twin sons. They're seniors in high school! I thought nannies were for children. Mr. Wyndham is a busy man and wants a stand in mom to address issues at the school as well as attend all sporting and academic events in his place. There will be other duties around the house that could be assigned later in addition.

Hey, it's easy money. I'll take it. It still leaves plenty of time for me to do my school work and fuck the hell out of my boyfriend while keeping my student loan cost down. This school year's salary will get me out of college debt plus put money in the bank. I also get to live in the guest house for free! Jake and I won't have to sneak around and have sex in the back seat of his car any more. We'll have a bed to destroy each other's body in over and over. It's a dream job really.

I dressed professionally in a classy, albeit modest pant suit as the agency suggested. The butler who gave the interview quickly explained there was no dress code.

If I got the position, I could dress however I normally did. Mr. Wyndham only made a brief appearance during it, leaving the decision to his butler. I didn't even know who he was until he left the room. He gave me a lingering once over then an almost unnoticeable nod to the butler before sharply turning on his way out.

Curtis, the butler, explained who he was and insisted Mr. Wyndham approved of me which was great news. He apparently hadn't liked any of the other women who had interviewed all week. Sure could've fooled me. Wyndham looked like an old, sour, asshole who didn't like anyone or anything except his money.

Things were going well while covering all the basic questions. Typical stuff I expected like how to handle emergencies. In the end, Curtis told me there'd be additional work for me since there wasn't a whole lot to do where being a nanny was concerned. Wyndham wanted to make sure his boys had someone present for them at games and other events for the most part. Maybe a little homework help if they needed it, but they did have tutors. It sounded easy.

I asked what other duties might be involved in addition to the teenagers. Surely, Wyndham had a maid because I wasn't signing up to wash pots and clean toilets. Fuck that.

"Glad you brought it up," Curtis answered with a wry smile. "There's a number of things Mrs. Wyndham did around the house. We'd need you to fill in some of those roles as well. We'll need you to sort of audition or have a test run, if you will, to make sure you will work out."

"Okay," I naively said. "Like what?"

That's when this six foot tall, lean, middle aged man stood up and unzipped his pants. I was stuck like a deer in headlights. Part of me wanted to run away. I knew it was wrong. Oh, it's wrong for so many reasons. Sex isn't supposed to be involved with getting a job. This isn't Hollywood. There shouldn't be a casting couch. And I've never cheated on Jake. Mostly, I was curious about the hard cock he whipped out in front of me. I've never been with anyone else, and I've often fantasized about what it would be like with other men.

Curtis noticed my hesitation. I guess you could call it that. It was more like shock than anything. "Wyndham was always too busy to take care of his wife's needs. He didn't care to make sure she was fulfilled. You can't throw money at a pussy and expect it to orgasm."

I had to bite my lip. That was pretty funny.

"It might have started with us taking care of her, but we all got more than just a little used to the perks of the job. Any stand in for her is going to have to pick up where she left off. It's been over three months now. We're all horny and in need of some serious action."

I wondered who the "we" were that he was talking about. Mr. Wyndham was loaded. He had to have a mechanic, cook and maid in addition to the butler. How many more people were on staff? A gardener, maybe? This job seemed like it would be perfect, but I can't be expected to sleep with everyone. The home workers were probably female. They might not be included. What was I doing? I wasn't actually considering this was I?

"Look, Lace, suck it or leave. I

have more interviews lined up."

It's just a blow job. Technically it's not cheating if it's only oral. That's what I convinced myself. If I got the job, I might have to give at the most three guys a blow job from time to time. It wasn't ideal, but I could live with it.

I reached out and took his cock in my hands. It was about five inches, but man, it had a decent thickness to it. As soon as he was in my hands, Curtis reminded me, "Don't forget. This will determine who gets the job and who keeps checking the employment ads."

No pressure there. Thanks. I hadn't thought about it from that angle. I could wind up cheating on Jake for nothing if I don't get it.

Better make it the best blow job of my life. Luckily, I don't mind sucking dick, and I love the taste of cum unlike most girls my age.

I ran my tongue around the head of his cock slowly to get it wet. Sucking Jake off was second nature to me now, but suddenly, I felt like I'd forgot everything he ever taught me. This was the most important blow job of my life. I needed this job.

I run my tongue along the shaft to get him lubed up before sucking the head into my mouth. Eye contact. Always eye contact. I looked Curtis in the eye before lowering my head to take his full length and heard a small noise escape his mouth like a soft groan.

Good. He liked that.

Pulling back, I wrapped my hand around the base of his cock giving him an expert squeeze. I slid my mouth up on his cock until my lips were behind the head and ran my tongue around it while sucking hard. Then I started stroking him and twisting my hand around his shaft while bobbing my mouth down to meet it. I'd alternate taking his full length into mouth and sucking hard as well.

It didn't take long until I knew my work was about done. I reached out with my free hand to cup his balls, and he groaned loudly. I felt them pull up tight against his crotch. He'd be coming soon. I didn't break eye contact and continued to look at his closed eyes after he squeezed them shut until he had completely unloaded in my mouth. Pushing my lips back to the root of his shaft, I milked every last drop out of him and licked him clean as I released my mouth's hold.

I sat there feeling hot as ever and waited to see what happened next. It was a sore disappointment. Curtis zipped his pants and thanked me for coming. How lovely. "We have more interviews scheduled this afternoon. We'll let you know by the middle of next week," he said, walking to the door. He opened it and waited for me.

When I walked through the doorway, he asked, "You remember

your way out?" The door closed behind me immediately after he finished speaking, not giving me a chance to answer.

I have never been so humiliated. I felt tricked and used. I drove the whole way to my parents' house fighting back tears. There's nothing I could do about it either without admitting to Jake that I cheated, and for what? A stupid job!

My parents were already home, so I went in through the side door to sneak up to my room. I knew Jake would be waiting for me to tell him how the interview went. Up in my room, I took a few deep breaths to steady my nerves before calling him. I pulled out my phone and saw a missed call and voice mail from a strange number. Anything to delay trying to hide how upset I was from my boyfriend was welcomed right then, so I listened to the message.

It was Curtis, Mr. Wyndham's butler. I got the job! They wanted me to start on Monday, and I could begin moving into the guest house that weekend.

I sat on the edge of my bed with my mouth dropped open in surprise. I couldn't believe it. I actually got it! But now I wasn't so sure I wanted it with all the stipulations that came with it.

Chapter Three

Dear Diary,

Jake helped me move into the guest house today. He wanted to get a look at it as well as learn how to access it on the property when he came to visit. Turns out, it won't be that easy. The property is secured, and it would be frowned upon for me to have visitors showing up at the gate trying to gain entry often. If he used my access card to get in on his own, they would see it on the cameras, and I'd be terminated immediately. The only way for him to visit is if he rides along with me when I come home. It'll work, but it means no surprise quickies.

There wasn't much to move in since the guest house is furnished. We brought my school books, laptop, and a couple baskets of clothes along with a few other accessories. I packed in a hurry, and there would be plenty I'll remember I need that I'll have to bring on my own later. We just wanted to get here to break the house in as soon as we could.

That was a good thing too because no one told me there would be a party at the estate. The guard in the shack frowned when he learned I was moving in, but when he saw the meager possessions I had brought, he waved us through.

He issued a stern warning that we were not to wander from the guest house and make as little noise as possible. It was the twins' eighteenth birthday, and Mr. Wyndham would not be pleased if there was even the slightest interruption.

Other than a couple times when we found an opportunity to have one of our houses to ourselves for a few hours when we were both free, every time he and I had ever been together was cramped up in the backseat of his car. My old bug was too small to even attempt it. We tried being romantic once and laid a blanket on the ground out in the country out of view from the road. A wayward snake decided to join us and guaranteed I would never attempt outdoor sex again. Little did I know that would soon change.

But now we had this whole house to ourselves. I could have visitors as long as they arrived and left with me. There would be no end to our fuck fests from now on. The thought of having Jake to myself on a bed for as long as I wanted him had been the only thing I could think about since learning I got the job yesterday. The thoughts running through my mind kept building, and the fantasies about it made me so horny I could burst if I didn't have him inside of me soon.

That's why as soon as I walked into the guest house door, I threw my basket on the floor and grabbed him. He was still holding the second basket that had a full book bag on top and was trying to pull back from me. I think he was trying to tell me he needed to set it down first. There was no time. My needs were urgent. I pushed against it with my hip hard and long enough he finally took the hint and let the basket drop.

Jake put his hands on my waist and carried me into the center of the room turning around trying to decide where to go. The living and kitchen areas were divided by a couch placed in the open room in such a way that the back of it acted as a short wall. He walked me over to it, and spun me around, laying me over the back of it.

My short skirt hiked up on its own when he folded me over the couch. Jake spread my legs apart and ran his fingers along my already wet pussy. He didn't waste a minute. I heard the sound of his jeans unbuckling, and he grabbed hold of my panties, moving them to the side. Within seconds of him setting me down, I could feel him inside me.

His size was immense and entering me like that without warning made it rougher than I usually like it. My feet flailed about trying to find some footing to brace myself, but they couldn't reach the floor. I was completely at his mercy. He was thrusting into me so hard the couch moved forward from his force.

The hold he had on my shoulders kept slipping which threw off his rhythm. He switched it up putting one hand around to cover my mouth. A trick he knows I like. Thrust after thrust kept banging into me harder and deeper. I could tell he was getting close while I was just getting warmed up.

Finally, he grunted, and I could feel him release his load. I love the way his hard cock swells even larger just before release. It's hard to believe I can take all of him to begin with, but then he gets even bigger. He collapsed onto my back, his breathing short and raspy.

I looked up and saw a face in the window. As soon as I saw him, he disappeared. I didn't know who it was, but he was young. He was probably one of the party guests who had wandered over exploring the grounds. I wasn't sure what to do. If I reported it to someone, there was a good chance I would be in trouble for not making sure my boyfriend and I couldn't be seen. I definitely couldn't tell Jake. He'd for sure take off after the guy ready to give a beating first and ask questions later.

"I'm sorry, baby," I heard him mumble. "I'll take care of you. I promise. I couldn't help myself. I've been thinking about having you anywhere at any time I want ever since you told me you got this job. I couldn't wait."

It made me smile hearing his promises to please me, but I already knew Jake would reciprocate. He was normally a very attentive lover, so he was allowed a selfish spurt from time to time.

We peeled ourselves away from each other and the couch. It was angled weirdly several feet from where we had started, but Jake had it back in place in no time.

He came to me, and I couldn't believe he was ready to go again so soon. Crushing his mouth over mine, he walked me backward down the hall, opening doors as we went. There was a spare bedroom, but the bed was in pieces on the floor. Jake groaned. It wasn't a good sign. We passed the bathroom and a closet before finding the main bedroom with its own master bath. The shower was built for two, but looked like it could easily hold several more bodies at one time.

Luckily for us, the bed was put together and was even made, not that we would have concerned ourselves with sheets at this point. When the backs of my legs hit the bed, he stopped. He reached for the bottom hem of my shirt and lifted it over my head exposing my breasts which were barely contained inside my bra. The skirt I was wearing he shimmied down my legs until it lay crumpled at my feet.

Expertly, he unfastened my bra, leaving it to hang while he playfully pushed me back onto the bed. He lifted my hips and yanked my panties down my legs until he tossed them across the room. I shimmied my bra off my arms and threw it to the side as well.

Lowering himself next to me, he propped himself up on one elbow and slid his hand between my legs. Soon his fingers were inside of me. One at first, testing to see if I was ready, followed by a second. He thrust them in and out and twisted them around the way he knows will drive me crazy. When my breathing deepened, he found my clit with his thumb and began driving it in small circles around and around. Once I was about to my limit, he forced a third finger inside me to help bring me to climax.

"Damn I love your job," he whispered, as my cum ran down his fingers to his wrist.

Jake stood and undressed quickly kicking the clothes to the side. "Your turn," he said, climbing into the bed and laying on his back.

I was already close to being worn out, but I crawled up next to him. Bending over his hard cock, I took the full length of it in my mouth to lube him up. Then I straddled him, and guided his shaft inside me. I almost came straight away. He's huge, and my body was ready.

Slowly at first, I grinded my hips into him, reveling in the sensations being filled to the brim made me feel. I started moving faster and faster trying to bring him to the brink with me. It was a lost cause. I came several times over before he was ready.

I could tell he was getting close. He always squeezes my hips hard and starts guiding me on top of him when he's about to release. I threw my head back to prepare, and when I did, I saw that same face in the window again. I let out a gasp then quickly glanced at Jake. If he heard me, he paid no attention, probably thinking it was from the ecstasy he was causing me.

Jake released his load, and I could feel it spray inside of me. I climaxed too, and I could feel myself tighten and release around his cock while I sprayed down over him like a waterfall.

When we were spent, I fell into his arms trying to catch my breath. As I lay there, I made a note that curtains were the first thing on my list for this house.

I would've been content to fall asleep in his arms. It was one thing we'd never been able to do. In fact, I was almost out when he gave me a quick shake to stir me. Blinking open my eyes, I looked at his gorgeous face.

"C'mon, babe," he said. "Let's get cleaned up."

There was no resisting. He pulled me up, and I followed him into the bathroom a little unsteady on my feet as my legs were still weak and shaking. Somehow he had the energy to break in the shower before practically carrying my worn out body to the front of the house. He laid me on the table proclaiming he was hungry and demanding to be fed.

He ate me for close to an hour. I lost count how many times I came. Near the end, I looked across the room. It was later in the day, and the sun was going down. There was still enough light that I could make out that same face in the window. In my weakened, sex delirium I actually thought I saw two.

Chapter Four

Dear Diary,

I'm afraid I may get fired before I really even have a chance to start this job. Mr. Wyndham doesn't seem to like me at all. Why did he even allow me to be hired?

Yesterday was the party which meant I had to stay at the guest house. That was easy to do with Jake having his way with me over and over again. I decided to explore the grounds today. My duties don't actually begin until tomorrow, Monday, but I felt like it was better than staying in the guest house being bored.

I first ran into him near the flower garden on the far side of the house from where I stay. He took one look at me and crumpled up his nose. The butler was close by, and he immediately began a heated conversation with him. I was too far away by that time to hear what was being said, but when I glanced back, I could see the disapproval on his face. Plus, he kept pointing angrily in my direction.

A couple more times, I crossed his path while I was out. Each time, he gave me a disgusted look, and one time he asked, "Who taught you how to dress?" before storming off.

I thought I looked good in my shorts and tank top. It had been explained that there was no dress code, and I could wear everything I normally wear. If that wasn't the case, someone needs to tell me before I lose my job over something as dumb as a clothing mistake.

It was that comment that sent me back to the guest house, but I was far off on the property at the time. I looked around and decided the quickest way back was to cut across the lawn toward the garage then walk the path from there. That was probably something Mr. Wyndham would make a fuss about too: walking across the lawn. I didn't care. Honestly, I didn't. Fire me and get it over with already.

As I made my way past the front of the garage, all the bay doors were open. Each slot was filled with some fancy car or another. Noises could be heard coming from within. Clinking and clanking of tools left a shrill echo vibrating outside. There was no one in view.

I was almost to the far side of the garage when I heard a voice call out my name. "Lacey!"

I stopped and turned, but I couldn't see where the voice was coming from. Just before I was about to continue walking, I heard him again.

"You're Lacey, right?" a man said, stepping out from the front of one of the parked cars. He wiped his hands on a rag which he threw over his shoulder. "The nanny?"

"Yes," I said, taking a couple

steps toward the bay before stopping.

The man laughed heartily, "You can come in. I won't bite."

I walked into the garage, and then he added, "Unless you ask me to."

His words jolted me, and I whipped my head to look at him directly. He was eyeing me up and down, and the look in his eyes told me to run. It also made my pulse start thumping on my lady button. My body liked how he was sizing me up even if I wasn't sure I did.

"The name's Frank," he said, holding out a hand. He pulled it back quickly raising it up to show the grease and muck. "Sorry."

"Nice to meet you," I said,

taking a step back.

"Leaving so soon," he asked, reaching into a cooler. He pulled out two beers, and handed one to me.

I looked around nervously, not sure this is what I should be doing.

"Don't worry. Wyndham almost never comes out here. It's too dirty," he said in a mocking voice.

Reaching for the beer, he handed it to me, but not before opening it first. I took a sip, and he guzzled about half his can.

"What's your rush? Can't spare a little time for us to get acquainted?" The way he asked that question implied he wasn't interested in learning about my hobbies.

The garage was huge, and there were several support posts inside. One wasn't more than a couple feet from me. I walked backwards until I could lean against it, sipping my beer. We were in full view from the outside. Not that anyone was nearby. I thought there was no way Frank would try anything when we could be spied so easily.

"I was wondering when you were going to get to me," he said.

"What're you talking about?"

"You're making the rounds, right?"

I still had no clue what he was trying to say.

Frank walked over to me, and flicked one nipple. "You know, introducing yourself to the staff."

Instinctively, I crossed my arms over my chest, and said, "No, that is not what I'm doing."

"Well, Curtis did explain what all your duties included, didn't he?"

I thought back to the day of the interview when he went into detail about how Mrs. Wyndham had slept with the staff regularly, and they expected the nanny to take her place in fulfilling their needs. I knew what I was getting myself into by taking this job, but I also thought it'd be something I'd have some say in as well. Shouldn't I have some say in who I slept with?

He unzipped the front of his overalls, and unfurled his semi-hard cock. "Don't worry, babe. I'll make it quick. I'm behind on my work already," he said, pulling my hand down to start stroking him. His cock stiffened up fairly quickly.

Frank crushed my mouth hard with his. I could taste the alcohol he'd been drinking since long before I arrived. The whole time he kept my hand on his dick, stroking himself with it. Once he was hard, he told me, "Drop your shorts, babe. You're in for a treat."

I let them fall around my ankles. I wasn't wearing anything underneath them. He bent me over the hood of the nearest car, and entered me. Taking me like that without any warm up pretty much guaranteed I wouldn't cum. Since I knew I wasn't going to enjoy it, I hoped it ended fast.

He fucked me slowly. Every deep stroke in, he'd moan. "Oh, baby, you're so tight. I could fuck you all day, baby. Your pussy feels so good. Curtis made the right decision hiring you."

His words did excite me. I had never been talked to like that. If he kept talking and lasted long enough, I might actually cum. Then I heard the sound of crunching gravel as someone approached, and I knew we were about to be busted. That sent shivers of excitement through me, bringing me close to the edge of climax.

Curtis walked into the garage, and asked, "You started this party without me?"

He walked over to us and

tapped Frank on the shoulder. "I'm tapping you out, buddy. Move to the other side."

They angled me over the hood, so Frank could shove his hard cock down my throat while Curtis took over fucking me from behind. Soon after Curtis started plowing into me hard and fast, I could feel him spit down my ass. I wasn't sure what the wetness was I felt at first or why.

Then he pulled out and pressed the tip of his cock against my virgin asshole. I couldn't object because my mouth was filled with Frank's cock. I flailed my hands about behind me to press on Curtis' legs, trying to move him away.

Curtis backed up and asked,

"Do you want me to stop?"

Frank pulled back, freeing my mouth to speak.

I had always wanted to try anal, but had been too nervous and scared. Jake's cock was large, and I worried he might rip me open if I let him. If I was going to try it, Curtis was a nice trial size to experiment.

"I don't want you to stop," I told him.

"Alright. Frank, keep her mouth full. We don't need her screaming."

He didn't need more encouragement. Frank had his stiff dick in my mouth with both hands on the back of my head, thrusting it far down into my throat.

I felt Curtis press his tip against my ass again until he started to enter me. The pain was intense, and I would've cried out if it weren't for Frank keeping his dick shoved in my mouth. Curtis continued to press forward slowly, releasing a low soft moan that turned into a growl by the time he was completely inside me. Once he made it past my tight ring, the pain lessened. It was even almost enjoyable.

He slowly went in and out, allowing his full length to re-enter my ass each time. Every minute or so, he'd spit on me again to keep me lubed. The slow and steady movement of Curtis from behind me in no way matched the furious thrusting of Frank who kept trying to lodge his dick deeper into my throat, telling me how great I was at sucking him off.

Curtis reached his hand around and started playing with my clit. The stim play coupled with an ass full of cock felt amazing. Within a couple minutes, I felt myself coming hard. My juices ran down my inner thigh and on down my leg. Over and over again, he made me cum by perfectly timing his thrusts with how he was rubbing my clit.

Frank dropped one hand from my head and started squeezing my nipples with it. First one then the other. I had never received so much pleasure without a cock in my pussy before, and it made me long for a third one to know how it felt to be completely stuffed.

I could feel Frank getting close, and I braced myself for the load I was about to taste. Just before he came, he pulled back and positioned the tip just in front of my face. Stroking himself, he shot his wad into my open, wanting mouth. I could feel him spray all over my tongue and the inner walls of my cheeks.

Soon after, Curtis was ready to blow. He had been offering me slow and steady strokes since he began. When he was about to cum, he grabbed my waist, and started thrusting into my ass hard eliciting loud cries from me until he clamped one hand over my mouth while he continued to fuck me. I could feel his cock vibrating against the tight walls of my ass as he unloaded inside of me.

Curtis pulled out, and I bent down to grab my shorts. Pulling them back up, I fastened them and straightened them out as best I could. They were dusty from laying on the floor of the garage at my feet, and I brushed as much of it off as I could. The white tank top I wore was covered in grease smears from Frank's hands. It would have to be tossed. I didn't bother tucking it back in, knowing I would be back at the guest house in just a few minutes after I left.

Once I was dressed again, I

looked around. I was alone, or at least I thought I was at first. There were noises coming from a couple cars away. I peeked around from where I was standing and could see his legs sticking out from under a Cadillac where he was already back to work. Curtis was nowhere in sight. I had never felt more used, but it thrilled me at the same time.

As I walked back, I ran into Mr. Wyndham again. He looked me over from head to toe, and frowned at my now ragged appearance. "Please be aware that you are expected to maintain at least the basic grooming habits while in my employ," he snorted before walking away.

Once in the guest house, I

immediately jumped in the shower. My cum had dripped down my legs and into my sandals by then. The only thing I saw in the garage to try to clean myself with were the greasy rags Frank used on his hands, and I didn't want to put them anywhere near my pink, perfect pussy.

In the shower, I thought about everything that had happened since I took this job. There was the great sex with Jake, but we had an uninvited audience. Curtis had his way with me twice, and now the mechanic as well. The best part of this job was the amazing sex, but it was also the worst part.

Chapter Five

Dear Diary,

Monday night was my first official working day as the "nanny." Hard to believe I have that title for a pair of adult twins. There was an informational meeting at their school that night for the Debate Team. This would be their fourth year, but they were still required to attend. Frank acted as driver, not just mechanic. He took the twins to and from school most days, but I was expected to take them when Frank wasn't available and also to their extra-curricular activities.

Mr. Wyndham had issued a

memo to me after seeing how I looked Sunday. It was an official dress code for how I was to look whenever I was at the school or a school function. Luckily, I had a few outfits that would work without having to make a shopping trip. The light green sundress I was wearing should have past his inspection if he had seen me.

At the school, I didn't do much, but try to stay out of the way. The twins acted rather indifferent around me. They wouldn't introduce me even when someone asked about me. It was rude and insulting, but I tried to put myself in their shoes. They were far too old to have a nanny. They could've introduced me as anyone they wanted from driver to household assistant. It wouldn't have mattered to me. Anything would have been better than the cold shoulder they were offering.

When everything was finished, they gave me directions back to their estate. It was my first time driving in this area of the city, and I felt confident I could find my way back. Still, it was nice having the help from the boys.

It was close to ten when I realized we were lost. The road we were on ended at a closed gate in front of a large, fenced field surrounded by trees. I put the car in park and dug my phone from my purse. "Let me try to figure out where we are," I told them, hoping this incident wouldn't get me in too much trouble with their dad.

"We know where we are," Lincoln said, getting out of the car.

"We're home," Landon said, joining his brother outside.

I looked around, but nothing seemed familiar. The boys entered a security code on the keypad, and swung the gate open before walking a ways into the field.

Turning the car off, I went after them to see what was going on. "Wait up," I said, following them into the field. "What do you mean you're home?"

"This is the back of the property," Landon explained.

"It's where we practice shooting," Lincoln added.

At least I wasn't completely lost. "Why did you have me bring you out here instead of the main entrance?" I asked, thinking they might just want me to drop them and go.

"We saw you," Landon said.

Lincoln walked closer and circled around me, brushing at the skirt of my dress as he went. "Last Saturday"

Landon came over as well. "During our party."

These boys were the faces I saw in the windows while Jake and I broke in the guest house. I recognized them as soon as we'd met, but I had hoped it was something they would never mention. With the curtains I hung, they wouldn't be able to peep me like that a second time. "You did?" I asked. My voice faltered, and I hoped they couldn't tell I already knew it was them.

"Yes," said Lincoln, "and we liked what we saw."

Landon was behind me then, and he reached down to the hem of my dress. Slowly, he started to pull it up my legs. "We thought we might enjoy a turn ourselves."

"That wouldn't be right, you two. I'm your nanny."

"Like we need a nanny," Landon scoffed.

"We're eighteen," Lincoln said, stepping closer.

By now, Landon had lifted my dress till I was completely exposed from the waist down. Both of them were pressed up against me, and while I didn't think it was the best idea to sleep with the boss's sons, I couldn't control the heat and excitement that was building within me.

"The only reason our dad hired you was to keep everyone happy," Landon said.

I was about to protest and tell them to get in the car.

"And that includes us," Lincoln added, reaching out and pulling my panties down to my feet.

My mouth dropped open, and Lincoln began kissing me, awkwardly forcing his tongue around my mouth. He thrust his fingers against my clit and rubbed it hard. Pushing him away, I ordered him to stop.

The look on his face was outright comical. It was easy to see neither of these boys were used to being told no. "You're doing it all wrong," I told him gently.

I reached out and took his hand, guiding it back to my crotch. "You can't go straight for the clit without a little warm up first. It can be almost painful if you do it too soon."

Keeping my fingers over his, I guided his hand around my pussy. I showed him how to softly stroke the outer lips and gently insert a finger just a little ways inside. His brother Landon was slobbering on my neck trying to kiss me seductively, but there was only so much I could teach in one night. Once I felt my desire start to rise, I brought Lincoln's hand back to my clit and showed him how I liked to be played with.

We stood in the field like that for a few minutes. The boys tried their best to turn me on, and I helped show them little things to improve their style.

Soon, Landon couldn't wait anymore. He stepped away from me and undid his pants letting them fall to his feet. Laying on his back on the ground, he motioned for me to climb on top of him.

I chuckled softly at his eagerness, but I straddled over him and lowered myself on top of his hard shaft, guiding his cock into me as I went. I started riding him slowly, not sure how experienced he was or how long he would last. His eyes rolled back in his head, and he moaned every time I grinded into him.

Lincoln appeared next to me without his pants and shoes on. He was jerking himself off. Knowing what he wanted, I took over for him. I started stroking his dick and spitting on it to prepare it for my mouth. Once I had his entire cock wet, I opened my mouth and slid him inside. I'd only been sucking him for a couple of minutes when Landon pushed my ass away from him announcing it was his turn.

I leaned onto one leg waiting for

them to switch positions. I rode Lincoln's cock hard while sucking off Landon. It didn't take them long before they wanted to switch again. It wouldn't have been a big deal if we were in the car, or somewhere comfortable like a bed. The ground wasn't that soft, and I wanted to stop digging my knees into it.

Once I had Landon's cock inside me again, I told them to let me work them one at a time to get them off. I started riding him harder and faster. Landon moaned and squeezed my waist hard enough to hurt.

Lincoln didn't like standing on the sidelines watching his brother get all the action. He told Landon it was his turn and yelled at him to get up. Landon either didn't hear him or ignored him. Lincoln couldn't wait any longer.

He came around behind me and pressed me down flat against his brother. "What are you doing?" I asked.

I could feel him over me, but it was too dark to see anything when I angled my head back. Then I felt him. He was practically sitting on my ass. As soon as I realized what his intention was, I felt his cock forcefully penetrate my ass. I screamed out.

"Oh, you like that, don't you?" he asked, thrusting into my ass as fast as he could manage.

As painful as it was, it excited me too. Both holes were filled with cock. Landon was pumping into me from below, and his brother was ripping my ass open. "Yes!" I yelled. "Fuck me harder!"

It wasn't something they needed to hear twice. The boys gave me the fucking of my life. My cum dripped down over Landon, soaking him. My pussy violently constricted around him in a near constant climax. Being in sync like twins typically are, they came together. Both of their hard cocks swelled even larger, and I screamed out loud enough I worried the main house would hear me.

When we were through, we got back in the car, and they directed me to the front entrance. I pulled up to the garage where Frank stepped outside. He took one look at me and laughed, "I see the three of you introduced yourself properly."

"Something like that," I told him.

Landon and Lincoln ran off to the estate, and Frank leaned in. "Lucky you. I've been thinking about that ass of yours since I saw Curtis tear it up, but I'll let you rest and clean up before I go for seconds with you," he whispered.

Chapter Six

Dear Diary,

I've spent the last couple days holed up in the guest house keeping to myself, so there hasn't been much to write about. My poor bottom needed time to heal from back to back sexual adventures. After hearing Frank say he was interested in trying my ass on for size, I decided it would be best to stay away from everyone until I was ready just in case.

My nanny schedule was pretty sparse, so I thought it would be fine to spend time alone until I was needed again. I should've known that was too good to be true. I received an email late last night telling me I was to meet with Mr. Wyndham in his office Thursday morning at nine. Talk about short notice. What if I hadn't seen it in time?

It was a nerve wracking walk up to the estate. I knew nothing I wore would pass his approval, and I didn't care anyway at this point. Until I had a payday, there was nothing I could do about changing my wardrobe. Besides, I pretty much figured I was fired. By now, I was sure all the help knew about my tryst with the twins, and one of them probably let something slip to their dad. Actually, I wouldn't be surprised if one of those brats didn't tell him outright.

The email said I was to wait in the library in the main estate which made sense seeing as how the wing was private for family members only. I walked into the library, but it was empty. I took a seat in a chair by a window to wait. As soon as I sat down, I heard his booming voice.

"Miss Moore, I see you've made yourself comfortable," he said, sounding irritated.

"Mr. Wyndham," I said, jumping from my seat. "I'm sorry. No one was -"

He cut me off with the wave of his hand and sat at his desk then motioned for me to sit in the chair across from him. "I believe it's time we had an official meeting concerning your job duties and what is, and is not, acceptable behavior for you.”

This was it. He was going to bring up my tryst with his sons and let me go. I braced myself to hear him say I was fired.

“What exactly did Curtis tell you the job would entail?”

I opened my mouth to answer, but he didn’t give me a chance to speak.

“Never mind,” he said, giving me a disgusted look. “I’m sure I know exactly what he told you. I understand Lincoln and Landon do not require twenty-four hour attention, but you are still a full time employee. Monday through

Friday and every other Saturday, correct?"

I nodded even though my hours and shifts had never been fully detailed for me before now.

"There may be the occasional off day when your presence is needed as well. When my sons don't require your... services," he said with a snide look, "there is plenty of work around the estate you can help the rest of the staff perform. It's been brought to my attention you were nowhere to be found for the last two days. They will be docked from your pay, and if it happens again, you will be escorted from the property. Are we clear?"

"Ye-Yes, Mr. Wyndham. I'm

really sorry," I said.

"That will be all. You can show yourself out."

I stood up and began walking out of the room. "One more thing, Miss Moore."

I turned back to him nervously fidgeting with my hands.

"Sunday night, there is a dinner at the club. Frank will drive us, of course, but I need you to be there because my boys will no doubt become bored and want to leave early. Please find an appropriate outfit to wear. You won't be going inside, but that doesn't mean you won't be seen. Cover up. More is classy, Miss Moore. Less is," he paused, looking me down from head to toe, "trashy."

I hurried from the library and found myself almost running for the front door in no time. Luckily, I caught myself before heading back to the guest house where I would've hidden in shame the rest of the day. Regardless of how I might rant about not caring if I get fired, I couldn't lose this job. It allowed me to still attend my classes, live rent free in a gorgeous house, and the pay was amazing. The guest house was nicer than the home my parents owned. The sex so far had been a huge bonus even if a little over the top. I figured they'd just been without for a while, and it would soon start to taper off. Boy, I couldn't have been more wrong.

Instead of leaving the estate, I

wandered into the kitchen to see if I could be of use. No one was there. Strange. Surely, Mr. Wyndham had a cook. I started to roam the main house, steering clear of the library. I was looking in a bedroom on the second floor trying to find the maid when I was found by Johnny, the gardener. We had never met officially before, but he had been pointed out to me on my tour of the estate when I first arrived.

"Can I help you, miss?"

"I'm Lacey, the nanny. I was looking for the maid." I said, thinking it was he who needed help seeing as he was far from the grounds he was being paid to tend.

"I know who you are, miss," he replied, stepping into the room toward me.

The look in his eye told me everything I needed to know about what he was doing there. He wasn't lost or roaming the house aimlessly like I had thought. He was looking for me.

Johnny was devastatingly handsome. I'd seen him on the grounds almost every day. His uniform had to be uncomfortably hot to work in outside, but I'd watch him take his shirt off and pour water over his head and down his body before to cool off. He had muscles and outlines that didn't exist in real life. If there was anyone here I would've looked forward to trying on for size, it was him.

He walked to me and ran his

finger along the neckline of my shirt. "Are you needed somewhere right now?" he asked, barely above a whisper.

"The only place I'm needed is right here," I answered, trying to sound as seductive as possible.

His mouth clamped on mine forcefully, and he reached up under the back of my skirt. His hand was large enough to cover almost my entire ass, and he squeezed it hard enough to send a searing pain through it. Whipping me around, he awkwardly walked me to the bench at the end of the bed. Nudging the back of my knees with his own, they caved and bent onto the seat. He moved my arms forward until I was bent, ass up over the edge of the bed.

Not wearing panties made it easy for him to access all of me. Johnny brought his large, strong hand in-between my legs and stroked the full length of my wet pussy. Gripping my ass cheeks with both hands, he spread me open. I struggled to look behind me, but it was useless. I couldn't see him past my skirt that hung off my waist.

I felt his tongue slowly trace my butthole. The sensation startled me, and my instinct was to tell him to stop. No one had ever licked me there before, and the idea had always been unsettling to me. I had no idea it felt this good. Now that I was experiencing it, I found it thoroughly exciting.

Johnny licked round and round then darted his tongue into my ass. "Mmm, you taste so good. You like that?"

I couldn't form words, so I only moaned in response.

My head was down into the bed, and every time I tried to raise up, he'd push me back down. I couldn't see him, but I could hear his zipper being undone. It was followed by the unmistakable sound of clothing hitting the floor. He put his foot on the bench next to my leg, and spread my ass open again. I braced myself for another back door penetration.

Instead, he slowly slid his cock into my wet pussy, letting out one long, guttural groan as he entered me. The first few strokes, he took his time making sure to let me feel every inch as he drove deep inside then pulled completely out. I bucked my ass up to greet his cock each time. Dear God, he was thick!

Then he started pounding me hard and fast. Moans escaped my throat as I tried hard to swallow them. Mr. Wyndham could still be in the library not far from here. If he left, he would surely hear us with the door to the room wide open. As loud as Johnny was grunting, he could probably hear us from his desk.

Wriggling around, I turned my head to the other side and caught sight of a dressing mirror across the room. It was angled perfectly to watch Johnny as he banged hard against my ass. His cock was bringing me to my peak, and I screamed out, burying my mouth into the bed to muffle my cries. He showed no mercy and pounded my pussy even harder.

Looking back into the mirror, I saw her. Leaning against the door frame of the bedroom was Frieda. I'd never seen her before then, but I'd heard her name mentioned several times. She was Mr. Wyndham's maid. She had her hand underneath her uniform dress rubbing her clit as she watched Johnny fuck the hell out of me.

It was so hot seeing her get off

to the sight of us. My breathing quickly fell into sync with hers. I wasn't sure if she knew I was watching her too, but my next climax was linked to her. The closer she came, the closer I got. When her face tightened up and her shoulders quivered from the release, she sunk down to the floor. That was all I needed. I cried out again into the sheets of the bed. I came hard. My tight pussy convulsed all around Johnny's stiff cock while my cum soaked him and dripped down my inner thigh.

Not long after I came for the second time, I felt Johnny's cock engorge, and I knew he was ready to cum. "Let me taste you," I said to him quickly.

He pulled out, and knocked me to the side with one hand. I lifted myself up to him and took him in my mouth just in time to feel him squirt down the back of my throat. He grabbed the back of my head and thrust into my mouth, making sure not to spill a drop. After he was empty, he pulled back and started getting dressed.

I took a quick look behind him, but Frieda was gone. It was disappointing. I didn't realize until that moment I had been hoping to continue with her next. Why limit my experimenting to the smorgasbord of men when there were apparently women on the menu as well?

Johnny fastened his pants and

looked at me as I lay spent, half on and half off the bed. "You will definitely be seeing me around," he said with a wink before leaving.

Minutes later, I dragged myself from the bed to head out. I didn't know where I was going when I walked out of the bedroom. When I made it to the stairs, I saw Mr. Wyndham standing outside the library door staring in my direction with a disgusted look on his face. Maybe that was just his permanent expression seeing as how it's the only one I ever see from him. It was as if he'd been waiting for me. I looked down briefly, fidgeting with my shirt to straighten it. When I looked back, he was gone.

Chapter Seven

Dear Diary,

Today is the day my boyfriend found out there was more to my job than just being a nanny to two high school seniors. He took it a lot better than I expected he would. That's because he already had a pretty good idea what was going on.

I picked Jake up and brought him over for a night of hardcore sex. As far as he knew, it'd been almost a week since I'd been laid. I was hoping to get a little ass play from him without clueing him in to anything that'd been going on. I got that and so much more with some unexpected help from Frieda.

Jake and I explored the rather large shower in the master bath for the second time. I laughed at him because we hadn't worked up a need to get clean yet, but he insisted.

The water hadn't a chance to thoroughly dampen my hair before his hands were roaming my body. The experiences I'd had since starting this job less than a week ago were great, but it felt wonderful to be with someone who knew exactly how to push my buttons again. My body recognized his touch the moment he laid hands on me and started aching for the release only he could bring.

I pressed my hands against the

wall between the two faucets, leaning over with my legs spread wide open for him. He sank to the floor and began eating my pussy expertly. Thoughts raced about how to get him to explore my ass, and I finally decided it would be best to just be direct with him. Reaching behind me, I let my finger trace the rim of my hole. When I heard him gasp, I knew he'd seen what I was up to.

"Think you can help me with something?" I asked him, pretending to be coy.

There was a long pause, and he stood up behind me. Jake leaned into me, pressing me flat against the wall. I could feel his stiff cock between my legs. "Are you asking me to eat your ass?"

I giggled. That's not what I meant at all. "No, silly. Maybe you can use your fingers to loosen it up a little for later."

Jake's brows furrowed together then he realized what I meant. His entire face softened into a large grin. "Yes, ma'am," he said. "I'll see what I can do."

Dropping back to the floor, he continued to make a meal out of me while penetrating my ass with his finger. He slid it in and out several times, and occasionally swirled his finger around, pulling back on the rim of my hole to stretch it wider. Soon he had two fingers inside and was struggling to add a third.

A sound barely drifted to my

ears above the noise of the two shower heads blasting on either side of me. It was faint and distant. I couldn't remember turning the television on when we arrived, but that doesn't mean I didn't do it out of habit. It was no real cause for alarm because I knew without a doubt I had locked the door of the guest house behind me. After our first romp in my new place, I wouldn't put anything past the twins. It had to be coming from the television or maybe someone nearby outside. Either way, I knew Jake and I were alone.

He was really getting into his work, and I could tell that what I had planned on offering him for dessert was about to become the main course. His tongue was wreaking havoc on my pussy while his fingers were demanding entry to my ass.

There was a noise that came from the direction of my room that took my attention away only for a moment. If I had been able to think about what could have made that sound for a minute, I'd have figured out it was the sound of my bedroom door closing loudly. The noise only jarred me from my thoughts for a second before Jake started to fervently flick his tongue against my clit bringing me close to the edge.

The door to the bathroom flew open, and Frieda stepped inside taking the scene in with a hard stare. Her tongue started to trace her lower lip, and I watched her hand start to slowly inch up under her dress.

That was the push I needed, and I came violently. My entire body shook, and Jake used one hand to support my ass and keep me upright. His mouth sucked on my pussy, savoring every last drop that flowed out of me. It was the biggest orgasm I'd ever had watching someone getting turned on by us.

Jake slowly stood behind me, and put his arm around my waist. My head was still turned toward the doorway where Frieda stood, but he hadn't noticed her yet.

"My turn," he whispered in my

ear.

I didn't answer him. I kept my focus on Frieda wondering what she'd do next and worried she'd bust me for my exploits with Johnny.

Finally, Jake followed my gaze and saw her standing there. He quickly turned sideways, using both hands to block his cock from her view. "What the hell?"

"So sorry, sir. I'm here to clean," Frieda said, stepping closer to the shower.

"Not now. Can't you come back?" Jake asked.

"It's no problem, sir. I'm here to clean," she repeated, pulling the zipper of her dress down.

From the corner of my eye, I

saw Jake's mouth drop as Frieda exposed her perfectly round breasts. She wasn't wearing a bra under her uniform.

"Uh, no. It-it's fine. W-we're fine," he stuttered, watching her step out of the dress.

Jake saw me looking at him and quickly closed his mouth. He was growing flustered as Frieda ignored him and kept coming closer to us.

I caught his eye and gave him a half shrug then nodded in her direction. More than anything it was the guilt I had from all the men I'd been fucking the last week, but I didn't see any harm in letting Jake in on some of the fun.

"You serious?" he asked.

I gave him a smile and walked to the shower door and opened it for Frieda who had already stepped out of her shoes. She shimmied her panties down her legs and kicked them to the side before joining us.

Frieda walked into the shower, and I stepped to the side to make room. As big as I thought it was originally was not as accurate as I hoped. Frieda kneeled in front of Jake while the spray from the showerhead rained over her. She grabbed his stiff member and stroked it slowly before lifting her eyes to meet his. With a sly smile, she said, "I clean for you now."

She took his cock completely in her mouth with ease. Even my mouth dropped at how easy it was for her to swallow him whole. I glanced at Jake, and his head was tilted toward the ceiling. His eyes rolled back in his head.

I had never thought of myself as a jealous woman, but honestly, it pissed me off watching him react to her. There was no room for me to object. My own indiscretions were far worse, and I was the one who invited Frieda to join us. There wasn't much room for me to do anything, but I wasn't going to leave them to have all the fun without me.

Squeezing my way behind Frieda, she pushed me to the side then unbent her knees and stepped backwards. Her body was folded at a ninety degree angle leaving me unable to move much at all. Turning as much as I could, I let my hands roam down around her ass and found the folds of her pussy lips. I explored with one finger until I found her opening and slipped it inside. She moaned, and I turned back one last time.

Jake's head was down, and he was staring at me with an intensity I'd never seen in his eyes before. I gasped at how extreme that one look was affecting me. Already, the quake started echoing between my legs signaling the need for him again, but I would have to wait.

I continued to explore Frieda's pussy with my fingers. The only experience I had to draw on was satisfying my own needs. I hoped the way I was massaging and probing deep inside her pleased her as much as it did me. I wouldn't have to wait long to find out.

It took only a few minutes before I felt her pussy explode, sending her juices flowing on to my fingers before running down her inner thighs with the spray of the water helping it on. I had never had much desire before to be with a woman, but in that moment, I wished we had enough room to be able to taste the torrents that flowed out of her.

Pulling my hand away, I brought my fingers to my mouth to suck off her cum. As soon as my fingers touched my tongue, I heard Jake groan. I turned to him, and let him watch as I licked them clean. His mouth dropped open, and the vacant look washed over his eyes. He was about to cum. Closing my eyes, I moaned as I slowly licked the last one. That did it. He grunted loudly, and I didn't have to open my eyes again to know he was fucking Frieda's mouth hard spurting every drop down her throat.

We all rinsed off in turn before leaving the shower. Jake tossed towels to us girls that were mostly ignored. Frieda walked me into the bedroom backward until my legs hit my bed. She grabbed my hair and yanked my head to the side then planted a kiss on my mouth that made my knees give out. I tumbled onto the bed with her on top of me.

For a few minutes, I marveled at the thought of having such a beautiful soft creature laying on my body. It's a stark contrast from the muscular, rugged men I'd been in the arms of lately. The smell of her skin was intoxicating. It was an apple and pear aroma that drove my sexual hunger even higher. Knowing I probably wouldn't have too many chances like this, I took control and threw her off of me onto her back. I straddled her and lowered my mouth to her soft breasts, teasing her nipples with my tongue.

While working each breast one at a time, my hand found my way to the delicate flower between her legs. I continued passed and rubbed her pussy gently until her breathing came in short, gaspy waves. Then I rubbed her clit the way I attack mine when I'm taking care of my own business. She moaned and bucked into my hand. It was like Jake was no longer in the room. He'd been completely forgotten by me.

I crawled back and maneuvered between her legs. The only experience I had with fingering a woman was my own pussy, and I had never ate a girl out. There's a first time for everything, and I thought I'd just repeat what Jake does to me. It was a little intimidating especially since Frieda seemed like the type who would bark out instructions if she wasn't being pleased properly.

Spreading open her lips with my tongue, I listened to her every breath for clues of what she liked. I licked the full length of her several times, savoring everything. Her taste, her scent, her feel...It was all intoxicating. Soon I was swirling my tongue deep inside her while rubbing her clit with my thumb. I was getting ready to insert a finger from my other hand when I felt someone grabbing my ass and lifting it high in the air.

Jake... I smiled. We'd completely ignored that he was still here. Frieda saw what was happening and bent her knees raising her legs in the air giving me room to spread my own legs apart for him. I felt the knob of his dick pressing against me, and I let out a long moan as he entered me slowly from behind.

His strokes started long and deep, but the sounds of Frieda and I urged him on. He started fucking me harder than he ever had, and I poured all of my pleasure into Frieda's sweet spot. I devoured her like I hadn't had a meal in days. The harder Jake thrust inside of me, the more intense I attacked her pussy which only made her moan louder. Her moans egged Jake on even more. It was one brutally delicious cycle.

Frieda came over and over again. Her juices covered my face

and dripped down my neck. Jake was getting close. He grabbed my shoulders, digging in to forcefully pull me back into him as he thrust deep inside me. My legs were shaking from all the times I had cum. They wouldn't support me now if my life depended on it. I felt his cock enlarge as he got close, and it sent me over the edge. I cried out loudly as he shot his load inside me. My orgasm timed perfectly with his. We collapsed on the bed next to Frieda, panting and trying to catch our breath.

Frieda only took a minute to rest before standing up and walking to the bathroom. Jake and I crawled up to the pillows and laid down next to each other, watching the bathroom door curiously. Both of us waiting to see what she was going to do.

A couple minutes later, she emerged, zipping up her dress. Her hair was still wet and clumped to the sides of her head. She paused as she headed out of the bedroom and said, "I come back and clean for you again. Yes?" Then she was gone.

Jake and I rolled toward each other with smiles on our faces. "That wasn't what I had planned for today," he said with a laugh. "Not that I'm complaining."

I smiled at him and gave him a long kiss. "Me either. On both counts," I agreed.

Jake laid back and stared at the

ceiling. "I have a confession to make."

Oh no. This didn't sound good. Panic swelled, and I feared he was going to tell me he enjoyed Frieda more. Where was all of this insecurity coming from?

"A buddy of mine from school has an uncle who works here. He's a mechanic. Frank? I think that's his name."

Fuck! Jake knows. He knows everything.

Jake continued, "When I told him about you getting this job, he told me about his uncle. He also mentioned what some of your job duties would be. I didn't believe it until he described your hip tattoo in detail based on what his uncle had told him."

"I'm so sorry. I should've told you. I just didn't know how."

He nodded as though contemplating my admission. "I wasn't sure what to do about it or how to ask you myself. Then this happened," he said, rolling back over to me. "If this is one of the perks of the job, I don't think I'm going to have as much of a problem with it as I thought."

"Really? You mean that?"

"Yeah, I mean we're young. We're supposed to be having fun. Sowing wild oats and all that."

"Well, enjoy it while it lasts. I have a feeling Mr. Wyndham will be firing me soon."

"Why is that?"

"It's clear he doesn't like me. He's mean and nasty to me all the time. I'm surprised he even let me have the job."

"Have you sucked him off?" Jake asked then laughed.

I glared at him then laid back and closed my eyes. Even if a blow job would save my job, I doubt he'd want one from me.

"That's why you offered your ass to me on a silver platter, isn't it?" he asked. "You felt guilty."

"That," I said, "and I've learned that I like it."

I opened my eyes just in time to see the look of shock come over his face. "When you grabbed my ass just now, that's what I was expecting. It was a surprise when you didn't make my ass yours."

He propped up on one elbow and kissed me. "Oh, I still plan on it. The night isn't over yet."

Chapter Eight

Dear Diary,

Mr. Wyndham is the biggest jerk I've ever met. It occurred to me today that I really don't have to worry about being fired because it won't take much more before I get fed up and walk out. There was nothing on my schedule for today. As much as I would like to lounge in bed all day to recover from last night's bang session with Jake, I had been informed that my presence is required daily regardless of how little the twins are in actual need of a nanny.

I toured the grounds slowly

because my body was still sore. It was enough for me to come into visual contact with two of the estate's four employees I already knew. There were a couple others I hadn't met yet. It wasn't necessarily a bad thing. It was hard enough keeping four of them satisfied without adding more who demanded my body for their pleasure. Even still, I found myself wondering about them often and what they'd be like when we did get around to introductions.

In fact, I was lost in thought about the cook and Wyndham's personal assistant when I almost walked straight into him.

"Miss Moore!" he yelled out.

I looked up with barely enough

time to stop before bumping into him. "Oh, hello, Mr. Wyndham," I smiled. "I apologize. I was lost in my head and not paying attention to where I was going."

"No doubt day dreaming about more ways to distract my staff from getting their actual work done."

Ouch. My smile quickly faded, and I started to walk past him when he grabbed my arm.

"I was on my way to find you," he told me.

I stopped and quickly glanced at him before staring at my feet again.

"Tomorrow's dinner at the club has been weighing on my mind. It would do neither of us any good for you to show up in the rags you usually wear and embarrass me."

Rags! How dare he? Just because they aren't the frumpy frocks women twice my age and without any sex appeal call fashion does not mean my clothes are cheap.

"Here," he said.

Mr. Wyndham was handing a credit card out toward me.

"Buy yourself something more appropriate. This isn't a gift, mind you. It will be docked from your pay."

I stared at the card not sure I believed what I was seeing.

Mr. Wyndham grabbed my hand and shoved the card in my palm hard enough I thought he might cut me. "Go find Frank. I'm told you've already become familiar with him," Mr. Wyndham said, twisting his face into a disgusted grimace. "He's expecting you."

With that, he began to walk away. I stood watching him leave torn between being excited about the shopping trip and mad as hell over his condescending attitude. At this rate, I'd spend my next twenty years in debt to this asshat with everything he kept docking from my check.

"Now, Miss Moore," Mr. Wyndham bellowed, not breaking his stride or looking back.

I sighed and started slowly walking toward the garage trying to decide if I wanted to keep this job or not. It dawned on me that I didn't have to use his card. I could buy a decent dress anywhere. There was a little money in my account. Surely it'd be enough to buy something appropriate for the dinner.

With this plan in mind, I quickened my pace. Frank already had a car backed out of the garage and was waiting for me to arrive. "Took you long enough," he said. "I was expecting you a while ago."

"Mr. Wyndham just told me to find you," I defended myself.

Frank shrugged. "Let's hurry. I have a lot to get done today besides taking you shopping." He walked to the driver's side of the car then added, "You can get your own door."

Walking to the car, I thought for a moment about sitting in the back seat, but decided I'd feel dumb if I did that. It would feel even more stupid when we arrived at the store, and I exited the back on my own. Climbing in the front seat, I told Frank, "You know I could drive myself."

"They probably wouldn't let you in the place if you pulled up in that little clunker bug of yours," Frank shot at me.

"What do you mean?"

"I'm not taking you to just any store. Mr. Wyndham's orders were crystal clear. We're going to Moreland's."

"Moreland's?" I repeated, feeling instantly nervous. It was the type of place celebrities shopped at, not someone like me.

Frank nodded. "And he called ahead. They're expecting you and have been told to dress you from head to toe."

We made it to the end of the long, spiraling road leading up to the estate. Frank made the turn to head into the city. "Including new panties," he said, turning his head to smirk at me.

There were miles of awkward silence after that before Frank spoke again. "When I saw you the other night, I thought you'd had fun with those twins. If I'd known otherwise, I'd have taken your ass right then."

I shot him a look not

understanding what he was saying.

"Yeah, I did my best to rile those two up about it. It's not hard to get them going, but they insisted you just took a tumble when they were showing you the shooting range. Nothing more."

Unbelievable. The only people at this place with a shred of decency are the two everyone would think should be the immature braggarts.

The rest of the drive I didn't say a word. Frank tried a couple more times to start a conversation, but I wasn't having it. It was bad enough that Wyndham repeatedly made me feel horrible by putting down my appearance, but now Frank knew I would be shopping for lingerie among other things. Not to mention, there was no way I could afford Morrisey Designs, not so affectionately known as Moreland to us commoners who couldn't drive past the store front without feeling their judgmental stares coming from within. I could only imagine what the final price tag on this would be.

At the boutique, the sales women actually treated be a thousand percent better than I had expected. They weren't fooling me. Mr. Wyndham had announced to them I would be coming, and they knew it was his money I was spending. They weren't being nice to me; they were ass kissing his credit card. Still, it made it easier that they knew exactly what I was in need of to help me find the right outfit.

Two hours later, I left the store with several bags and a receipt that would eat my paycheck for the next two months or more. My dress was beautiful. It was a simple black dress according to one of the women helping me. Yet, there was nothing about it that I would consider simple. It was black with a silver floral lacy material over it that added a beautiful accent. The best part was it was completely my taste, and I could actually wear it again.

I was also equipped with shoes, hose, a garter, panties and a bra. They had insisted on a bra fitting to make sure I got the right size. No matter how much I objected, they wouldn't let up. I gave in, and let them paw my breasts as they took the measurements they needed.

Frank was waiting outside, and he looked far from happy. "You could have told me this would eat the rest of the morning. I could've got some work done then came back for you."

His attitude was getting on my last nerve. "Didn't Mr. Wyndham tell you to wait for me?" I asked pointedly, putting my bags in the back seat.

That shut him up pretty quickly. It had been a guess on my part, but I was obviously right. How was I supposed to know it would take this long? Every dress I tried on was perfect as far as I was concerned, but the ladies kept bringing out more. It was like I was their doll, and they were playing dress up.

I was thankful for his silence on the way back. Tomorrow I would have to get decked out in this new outfit to do nothing, but hang out around the country club parking lot with the other drivers in case I was needed. It seemed like an absolute waste of my time and money for the outfit.

Frank pulled into the garage, and I couldn't wait to get back to the guest house. I had my hand on the door waiting to open it as soon as he came to a stop. I pulled the handle, but nothing happened. It was locked. I lifted up on the lock, and it went back down immediately. I turned to Frank and saw his finger resting on the automatic lock button on his door handle.

"Where do you think you're going?"

I really wasn't in the mood especially not with him. His cock was memorable, but his attitude today left something to be desired. "Let me out," I said sternly.

"Not until I've been compensated for my time."

I crossed my arms over my chest. "Doesn't Mr. Wyndham do that already on your paycheck?"

"Oh, if you aren't a pistol," he

said, unzipping his pants. "That's fine. I know exactly how to tame that mouth of yours."

Seeing his stiff dick peeking through the open zipper made my clit start throbbing with anticipation. It sucks how much the body can betray you.

"See how quickly I got you to shut up," Frank laughed. He reached over and gently pulled my arm until I slid over closer to him. "Now yank those panties off and climb up here," he ordered, lowering his seat back to give me more room.

I lifted my ass off the seat and pulled my panties down to my ankles and over my feet. I wasn't finished taking them off before

Frank was already grabbing my hips to lift me on top of him. He pulled me on his lap facing away from him. From behind, he rubbed my pussy gently.

"Mmm," he moaned. "You're already wet for me."

Little did he know, I generally was in a state of near constant arousal. I was always wet, but if it turned him on thinking it was all for him, let him think what he wants.

The limited space forced me to squat over him. There wasn't enough room for me to put my legs down around him. It didn't seem possible to me to be able to maintain this stance for long, but I figured we could start in this position. Frank guided the tip of his cock inside me then grabbed my waist and started guided me down his full length.

"Oh my god!" I screamed in a high pitch tone I almost didn't recognize as my own.

"Hits you deep, doesn't it," he grunted, grinding into me.

Whatever he was doing was both pure pleasure and almost painful at the same time. As enjoyable as it was, it almost made me want to stop. I'd never felt such a combination at once. I started to ride him being careful not to take his full length in when I went down.

"No cheating," he said, grabbing hold of me tighter. He started thrusting deep into my pussy from beneath, driving his full length into me hard every time.

Some foreign moan that was almost a high pitch squeal escaped my mouth in a constant tone. I had no control over the sounds I was emitting anymore just like I had no control over the fucking I was receiving. God, he was hitting me deep. I started to cum, and it was an orgasm that wouldn't end. He brought one hand down to rub my clit, and I thought I'd pass out from unbearable pleasure.

I came so hard, my legs were shaking within a couple minutes from when he started fucking me. This was the most intense I'd been plowed in my life. Soon, it was all I could do to stay upright on top of him. My legs were shaking so hard. I had one hand braced against the window and the other against the top of the car to support me. Frank just kept fucking into me harder and harder until he exploded his wad inside me.

"Damn girl," he huffed when he was spent. "I had my sights on your ass, but that pussy was so good, I couldn't stop."

With his help, I fell off of him barely able to catch my breath. My pussy was quivering, and I could still feel my own cum squirting out like aftershocks of an earthquake.

"That definitely made up for the trip to the city. You going to be alright?" he asked, squinting his eyes at me as I half lay across the seat.

"Yeah," I mumbled.

Frank laughed and zipped his pants. "Well you take all the time you need before you head on home. I'll put the windows down for you," he said, pressing the buttons to lower both front windows before getting out of the car.

I lay sprawled in the front seat for several more minutes until my breathing returned to normal. How is it something could affect me so wholly, but have him back to work so quickly and whistling along to the radio? Was it not as good for him?

As if he read my mind, Frank's face appeared in the open window of the door. "Doing alright?"

I nodded.

"Wore you out, did I?" he chuckled. "Anytime you're in the mood for another round, you know where to find me. That pussy of yours is the sweetest I've ever had the pleasure of tearing up." Then he was gone again.

I collected myself and got out of the car. I could hear him whistling from somewhere across the multi-car garage. He wasn't in view which meant he was probably on a creeper under one of the cars. I grabbed my bags from the backseat and started to head out.

"See you soon, Lacey," he called out, emphasizing the word soon. That one word made my clit ache with want, and I shook my head

wondering how many more times
my body's intense sexual desires
would betray me.

Chapter Nine

Dear Diary,

Today was the dinner at the country club. Nothing went according to plan, and nothing turned out the way I expected it would.

I was told Frank would be driving Mr. Wyndham and his sons to the club. I would be driving a second car there in the event the boys got bored and wanted to leave early. This way I could take them home while Mr. Wyndham stayed and enjoyed the rest of his night knowing handy dandy Frank was waiting outside whenever he needed him.

Translation? The boys would take advantage of this situation and leave early in the hopes of getting me alone again. I was so certain this was how the night would go, I had thrown a travel pack of wipes and extra panties in my purse for easy clean up afterward.

I arrived at the garage early. The last thing I needed was for Wyndham to wait on me even though I knew which car to take and had already been given the keys. It's not like he needed another reason to hate me.

Once I got to the garage, I found Mr. Wyndham was already there. He and Frank were deep in conversation. I could see a limo was pulled into the main circle drive of the estate which confused me because I thought Frank was driving the Cadillac tonight. Plans had changed, and I knew I wasn't one to be kept in the loop where logistics were concerned. As I neared them, Mr. Wyndham saw me approach. He gave me a long look from head to toe followed by a quick nod before turning toward the house.

Holy shit. Did he actually approve of me for once? I felt giddy, but stifled it inside as Frank walked over.

"Change of plans," he announced. "Wyndham hired a driver."

You've got to be kidding me. I'd spent hours getting ready making sure my skin was smooth from head to toe. I couldn't have the twins complaining to their dad that their nanny didn't have legs as soft as a baby's bottom. The thought made me laugh while I was in the shower. Not to mention, I was going to have to pay Wyndham back for this outfit whether I went to the club tonight or not.

"Looks like you're riding with me," he continued.

My mouth dropped open. I watched as Wyndham and his sons entered the back of the limo before turning to see Frank standing near the Cadillac. This made absolutely no sense. Why on earth would that man need three drivers in two different vehicles?

Frank read my expression wrong. "Don't be so upset about being stuck with me. I have strict orders not to touch you in that dress. You are to stay in pristine condition tonight."

He got in the car, and I walked around to the passenger side to join him.

"Maybe the twins have something in mind for you later," he joked.

"Oh, ha ha," I spat. "I just don't understand why I'm needed if there are already two drivers."

"That's what I'm saying. Maybe he wants you to turn his boys into men."

Frank guided the car out of the garage and started on the drive down to the road. "I'm just saying I wouldn't be surprised if they don't figure out what you're actually doing here and use it to their advantage."

He really didn't know yet. That was still a shocker. Of all the people at this estate, the only ones who can keep their mouths shut are the immature teenage boys. Who would have guessed? I had found it odd the Wyndham had never mentioned anything to me about it. Surely, he wouldn't be happy to learn about what transpired between the three of us. It wouldn't surprise me if he didn't fire me on the spot when he learned the truth of that night, and it had stumped me why he didn't mention it during our meeting in the library the other day. Then I learned why. If word hadn't made its way to the staff, maybe he didn't know about it.

We drove to the club, and Frank went straight to the parking lot. He greeted the gate guard, and we went right in. Once we parked, I started to follow him across the lot toward a small building where the drivers hung out while they wait. He slowed to a stop and looked at me concerned. "Listen, these guys..." his voice trailed off. "If they get out of hand, we'll hang out somewhere else. Just say the word, and we'll go."

That was unsettling. It made

me worry what I was in for once we went inside, but it felt good knowing Frank would look out for me. A dozen or so men were sitting around card tables in what could best be described as a shack. Typical rich people at a ritzy place not giving two shits about their employee's work conditions. The single room had a bathroom off to one corner, a counter with a sink and an old looking fridge with an out of order sign on it. There were two small oscillating fans on opposite corners of the room, and it was hot as hell inside. If I stayed for too long, my make-up would melt off my face.

As soon as I walked in, the guys began catcalling and teasing Frank about how he was supposed to drop the people he worked for at the door of the club not abduct them. It wasn't as bad as Frank had me thinking it'd be. One of the guys offered me a drink. On the floor in front of the fridge was a cooler. He opened it, and it was filled with bottles of water. "Courtesy of the club, and we should be ever thankful for their generosity," he said, rolling his eyes as he handed me the bottle.

I opened it and took a drink. It would be cooler to hang around outside. I was about to say something to Frank telling him I was just going to step out for air when his phone rang. I waited until he ended his call to tell him where

I was going.

"That was quick. Let's go," he said, putting the phone back in his pocket.

Frank headed out the door with me scrambling to keep up. "Go?" I asked. "That quick?"

"Yep, and he sounded irritated which means every second we shave off his wait time will benefit us."

We made it back to the car as quick as I could manage in these heels. I wasn't a novice to stilettos, but I was terrified of falling right now in this dress. If I had a hair out of place when Wyndham saw me again, it might mean my job.

I climbed into the passenger seat, and Frank didn't even wait for me to shut the door before backing out of the parking space. In less than two minutes, he pulled up to the main entrance of the club. Mr. Wyndham stepped outside, and Frank clambered around to open the door for him.

The whole evening was confusing. It was Mr. Wyndham who was ready to leave? Not the twins? Why were the two of us needed to drive one man home? Nothing made sense, but I knew better than to ask any of these questions out loud.

Mr. Wyndham got in the car, and Frank shut the door before heading back to the driver's seat. As soon as he was back behind the wheel, Wyndham barked out the order to drive him to the limo.

This night just keeps getting crazier. My anger rose up instantly, and I could feel it flush my cheeks. There was no need for this. The country club drive was spacious enough for the limo to drop him and his boys off. It was spacious enough for the limo to come back and collect him. Wyndham could've easily asked the valet to call for the limo's driver, but instead he had us pick him up to drive him all of three minutes just to get into a different vehicle. It was senseless, and in my opinion, showed only his arrogant and perverse abuse of his position.

Frank didn't say a word. He was a true professional. He never looked at me once during the drive probably knowing Wyndham could easily read his expression if he did. One quick sideways glance in his direction showed me the contempt he had written all over his face.

We pulled up alongside the limo, and Frank hopped out to open the door for his boss. Once Wyndham exited the vehicle with Frank shutting the door for him, I could hear voices. It was unclear what was being said, and honestly, I didn't care. I was looking forward to going back to the shack with Frank and hanging out with the other drivers. As hot as the building was, at least those were my kind of people. All of whom were probably underappreciated and taken advantage of by their bosses like Frank and I just were by Wyndham.

Suddenly my door swung open, and I jumped. It startled me enough I almost let out a small cry. Frank was standing there, and he motioned for me to get out of the vehicle. I had no idea what was going on or why I was needed.

I stepped out of the Caddy and turned to see Wyndham standing by the open limo door. "After you, Miss Moore," he said sternly.

Frank's face held not a single clue. There was nothing to warn me or prepare me for what was to come. I walked the few steps toward the limo.

"We have much to discuss concerning your employment with

me," Mr. Wyndham said.

This was it. The twins must have let something slip that clued him into our night in the meadow. Wyndham was mad that I soiled his boys, his pride and joy. I was about to be fired, but hey, I suppose it's not every day you get fired in the back of a limo. This would be a record story for years to come.

I got into the limo and sat facing the rear of the vehicle. Mr. Wyndham took a seat across from me. Once the driver was in the car, he was ordered to take the scenic route and drive around until instructed otherwise. Then, Wyndham closed the window separating the driver from the back.

Taking a deep breath, I braced myself for the news I felt was coming. I'd had this job for a week. I lost two days of pay for staying inside the guest house, and at least two months of pay for this dress. Instead of a severance check, I was going to be discharged with an invoice I'd have to pay.

"I am well aware it was explained to you that part of this position included taking over the duties my wife performed for the staff. I am sure something was said to you along the lines that I ignored my wife's advances forcing her to seek the attention of other men to fulfill her needs," Mr. Wyndham said directly.

I started to object. If I was being

truthful, I couldn't remember exactly what Curtis had told me the day of my interview, but I was fairly certain it wasn't put so coldly. Maybe it was.

Wyndham raised his hand to silence me. "I want you to hear it from me. It's not that I rejected her. That is false. No one man could have ever satisfied her. She had a desire lust that could not be quenched, but that being said, she did at least sleep with me. Unlike you," Wyndham said heatedly.

What he was trying to say clicked and hit me hard. That's why Wyndham had always seemed so short with me. I hadn't made my way around to take care of his needs yet. Somewhere deep down I summoned the courage to make a bold move. I carefully maneuvered across the limo to sit on the seat near him. "Is that why you always seem so disgusted with me?"

He furrowed his brows together. "I wouldn't say I've been disgusted, but I have wondered what it is about me that has made you not try to seek out my company."

"You're right in part. I was led to believe that perhaps you weren't even aware about what your wife was up to with your staff. But you're wrong about the rest. I haven't sought anybody out. They've been seeking me out repeatedly."

Mr. Wyndham's eyes widened

then his face softened. "I'll put an end to that immediately. No one should be coming after you like that. You should never be in a position to feel like you have to sleep with anyone at the estate. If you want to, and you seek them out, that's fine, but it's not a mandatory part of the job regardless of what you may have been told."

We sat near each other without a word for a few minutes before he spoke again. "Aside from that, how is the job going?"

I told him it was fine, but he must have detected the tone in my voice because he asked me again.

"Be honest, Miss Moore. The twins adore you, so I would hate to lose you as hard as it may be to believe given my recent behavior. Is there anything I can do to improve your working environment?"

"It's just that I feel I will always be working to pay off a debt," I confessed.

Mr. Wyndham raised his hand, and smiled. "Do not worry about all of that. You will be paid in full. There will be no garnishments on your checks."

I nodded as I processed what he was saying. Without the loss of pay, my job was as near perfect as it could be. The sex was thrilling and fun. It was becoming apparent I wouldn't always know when and where or even with whom it would happen until the moment was upon me. That mystery was tantalizing. It's not something I would want to cut out of my job description completely, but having a little more time to recuperate between sexual advances would be a positive change. Without really thinking about what I was doing, I placed my hand on his leg above his knee.

Wyndham stared at my hand for so long that I began to regret my decision to touch him. Maybe I had read everything wrong. When he was speaking, I thought he was telling me he was interested in sleeping with me too, but his reaction to my hand on his leg made me feel like I somehow missed something very important in the details. I was frozen in nervous fear. I didn't know whether to stand behind the move I made, or quickly yank my hand back.

Finally, he relaxed and leaned back into the seat, and reached one hand up to gently cup my face. "This look suits you. Sexy and sultry isn't always miniskirts and tight tops. Classy goes a long way in turning a man's head."

Noted. If I'm ever to try to seduce my boss after tonight, I need to dress the part apparently.

He leaned in and gave me a slow, sultry kiss. Wyndham was quite handsome now that I was up close and getting personal. His green eyes were like pools of jade which were a stark contrast to his sandy blonde hair. That square jaw of his made him always appear intense. Once his face softened, and he looked at me without glaring, he was quite an attractive man.

Slowly, he began guiding his hands up and down my body. The experience of his years was easily felt everywhere. He undressed me like a pro without any fumbling at all. Soon I was naked and sprawled on the seat.

Mr. Wyndham took his time, kissing every inch of my body while taking off his coat and tie. My clit was throbbing for his touch before he even began to unbutton his shirt. Many times I tried to assist him to strip him down faster, but each time, he brushed my hands away.

He sat up and took off his shirt before setting to work on his shoes. "Tonight is all about you, Miss Moore," he said in a husky voice while tossing his shoes on the seat across from us.

He stood as best he could in the back of the limo and slid his pants and boxers down in one motion revealing the largest cock I'd ever seen in my life. He had to be at least nine inches long, and his girth made me realize I should've packed lube in my purse as well.

I let out a gasp and didn't even care that my mouth was hanging open.

"Like what you see?" he asked, moving one of my legs so he could slide between them.

My eyes grew round. There were no words easily forming for me to say. I only knew it couldn't be possible for him to fit inside my tight pussy.

As if he could read my mind, he said, "Don't worry about a thing. You can take much more than you might realize."

Leaning back, he brought his mouth near my wet pussy as close as he could get without touching his lips to mine. I was prepared for him to begin eating me out, but instead, he only exhaled. That cool breath on my hot, throbbing clit sent waves of electrified, sensual energy coursing through me, and I moaned loudly.

Wyndham repositioned himself and touched the knob of his huge cock to the pulsating folds of my pussy lips. He stared deep in my eyes and slowly entered me.

He was massive, but I felt the walls of my pussy give way to his enormous girth. I couldn't believe I was taking him, and I lifted my head to look down. He was only halfway in! The visual caused me to shudder.

"I'll be gentle," he promised.

I looked up at him and confessed, "I'm so close." Breathlessly, I added, "I'm going to cum before you're completely inside me."

The devilish smile that formed on his face after I said those words hit just right, and I felt my body start to convulse. My cum drizzled down his shaft providing more than enough lube for him to finally enter me fully.

He bent one of my knees up and started rocking into me harder while he still maintained a slow rhythm. My orgasms kept coming until it was hard to tell where one ended and the next began.

I don't know how long he lasted, but it felt like an eternity before his cock swelled inside me. I let out a small cry not sure how I could manage to fit anything more in my pussy even just the slight addition to his girth as he prepared to cum. "Oh, Lacey," he moaned, spurting his cum deep inside me.

Wyndham collapsed on top of me out of breath for several moments before righting himself. He reached into one of the small compartments on the side of the limo and handed me a towel.

"Here," he said gently. "It appears we made a mess," he joked with a grin.

I took it from him, but didn't make a move to clean myself. I couldn't. There wasn't an ounce of strength left anywhere in my body.

He laughed. "I'll be ready again soon. For an old man, I have the drive of someone half my age. But, I know you need time to recover."

We started to wipe ourselves off and get dressed when he laughed out loud. "In fact, take tomorrow off. It may be difficult for you to move around in the morning."

It will take more than just one day before I'm able to walk without pain again. My one day off is easily going to stretch into two. Maybe even three.

Chapter Ten

Dear Diary,

Sorry I couldn't get to you yesterday, but I didn't get to bed until the wee hours of the morning. Plus, I crashed at the estate last night, so I couldn't have written anything even if I had the energy to put pen to paper. And believe me, I barely had the energy to breathe by the time I went to sleep.

I can't believe I've worked here for six months already! It barely seems like any time has passed at all since the fateful day when I had my interview and test drive with Curtis.

The staff held a small party for me last night to celebrate my anniversary. The twins were not invited much to their dismay. I'm honestly not sure if Mr. Wyndham ever learned about my one night romp in the meadow with them, but he did catch them planning to set up a rendezvous with me. He terminated my employment as their nanny immediately after that.

Since his personal assistant was preparing to move out of state at the time, he decided to just move me into that position. As his personal assistant, he made sure his sons knew I was completely off limits to them.

A new nanny was never hired to replace me. There was no need. I was brought in under the guise of the nanny title, but the main expectations of my job had nothing to do with childcare.

It's also hard to believe how much the staff has changed during this time. I know I keep hashing up the past in these pages, but I will keep saying it until I can no longer speak. Or write as the case may be. I was right to suspect something when Frieda joined Jake and me in the shower that day.

I had never been one to have jealous thoughts like that. The fact that I was feeling that way should've been my clue to alert me that something was off. Still, I was blindsided a month later when he left me for her.

Shortly after, Mr. Wyndham let her go for other reasons, but deep down, I know it was my broken heart that terminated her employment. The new maid hired to replace her is named Helga. She's much older and rather plump. She is never invited to any of the trysts that take place on the estate grounds. I get the feeling she wouldn't approve of them if she knew the truth about what was going on behind closed doors.

My anniversary party consisted of me, my boss, Curtis, Frank, Johnny and the cook, Miles. I've never been with the cook. Miles is a much older man who could easily be the same age as Wyndham's father. He never joined in with us, but he did enjoy watching from time to time.

The four of them took turns violating me with my full permission. They pleasured me over and over again for hours. Sometimes, I had all of them at once cramming every one of my sexual orifices with their cocks and leaving their cum dripping from my aching holes as they went.

As most things often do, the night started off slow with the occasional blow job or threesome. We'd continue to laugh and drink in between bouts in the bed of a spare room of the estate. By the end, they were all on me at one time for the duration.

It began with me giving Mr.

Wyndham a blow job. It was the first time he got into the action with his staff. Prior to that, I had only ever spied him lurking in the shadows from time to time watching. I wasn't sure he'd even participate tonight, and I was happily surprised when he finally did.

While I was sucking him off, Curtis laid down and maneuvered me over to ride him without me having to take my mouth off of Wyndham's cock for a second. Soon I felt the weight of another person joining us on the bed. It was Johnny coming to my other side for a hand job. After that, I wasn't the least bit surprised when Frank knelt behind and pounded my ass.

So many beautiful cocks. So little time and energy. They started to rotate. Each of them taking their turn and doing as they pleased with me. I had each of them every way possible more than once last night. When Wyndham made his way around to my ass, I almost ended the orgy immediately.

He leaned forward and whispered in my ear, "Do you trust me?"

That relaxed my nerves instantly. I heard the click of a bottle opening and knew he had lube to aid me. Getting that massive cock of his in my ass would be no easy task without it. Once he had me properly prepared, he actually slid his shaft completely inside me with ease.

My pussy burst in orgasmic pleasure. I had never been so filled. Johnny was underneath, bucking into my pussy, savoring the fruits of everyone's hard work as my tight walls convulsed and tightened around his amazing dick. Frank filled my mouth, and I jacked off Curtis while he made sure my tits weren't being ignored.

It was a night of many firsts. At one point, I even caught Miles jerking himself off while watching me get devoured by four cocks at once.

They had their way with me too many times for me to remember until I begged them for mercy. When all was said and done, I lay breathlessly on the bed while the room spun from the dizzying heights of pleasure I'd experienced.

Wyndham carefully and effortlessly lifted me off the soiled bed and carried me to where I would be sleeping. Last night was not only the first time I stayed at the estate, but in Mr. Wyndham's bed with him by my side.

Coming Soon
Nanny Diaries #2

Vicki Sweet didn't know what she was walking into when she took the job as nanny for the Rayburn's. Soon she found herself loaded with maid duties as well as chasing after the children while Lance worked and ignored all of his wife's illicit activities. Tori Rayburn needed to be put in her place, and Vicki was just the woman for the job. Chasing after Tori's affairs, Vicki began stealing them away one by one, but her eye remained on the ultimate prize. Vicki would have her saucy way with Lance before her job ended, and once she set her mind on something, she always got what she wanted.

More by Darling Coxx

Nanny Diaries #1

Lacey Moore bit off more than she could swallow when she took the position at the Wyndham estate. What was supposed to be the perfect job accompanied by great hours, pay and perks like living rent free in the guest house soon turned out to be more than she had could have ever imagined. The main duties of her job included making sure the entire staff stayed satisfied, and it was a job she intended on doing well.

About the Author

Darling Coxx is a seasoned writer who has been featured in many major publications under her given name. Taking a break from interviews and personal experience pieces, she is trying her hand at short novellas in the same genre she's been working in for most of her life.

Her adult entertainment career began while working as the manager of an adult store. It is her favorite position of any she's held, before or since. It was there where she made the contacts that allowed her to venture into the world of adult entertainment both in her own writing as well as producing a few pieces of her own.

Please feel free to reach out to her at DarlingCoxx@gmail.com. Follow her on Instagram @DarlingCoxx to stay updated on future publications. And don't forget to subscribe to her OnlyFans account @DarlingCoxx.